The Journey of Meng

A Chinese legend retold by Doreen Rappaport

pictures by Yang Ming-Yi

Dial Books for Young Readers New York

Pronunciation was prepared by Peter Liu of Rutgers University:
Meng Jiangnu — Mung Gee-ahng-new
Qin Shi Huangdi — Chin Shur Hwahng-dee

Published by Dial Books for Young Readers
A Division of Penguin Books USA Inc.
375 Hudson Street · New York, New York 10014

Text copyright © 1991 by Doreen Rappaport
Pictures copyright © 1991 by Yang Ming-Yi
Designed by Amelia Lau Carling
Printed in Hong Kong
by South China Printing Company (1988) Limited
First Edition
1 3 5 7 9 10 8 6 4 2

Library of Congress Cataloging in Publication Data
Rappaport, Doreen.
The journey of Meng : a Chinese legend /
retold by Doreen Rappaport; pictures by Yang Ming-Yi.
p.   cm.
Summary: A Chinese tale in which a woman goes in search of her
husband who has been forced to be a slave for a cruel king.
ISBN 0-8037-0895-5. — ISBN 0-8037-0896-3 (lib. bdg.)
[1. Folklore — China.] I. Yang, Ming-Yi, ill. II. Title.
PZ8.1.R2245 Jo 1991   398.22'0951 — dc20   90-19257   CIP   AC

*The art for each picture consists of an ink and watercolor painting,
which is scanner-separated and reproduced in full color.*

For Lyndie Callan,
and our journey to the other side
D.R.

For my mother and my son
Y.M.Y.

Meng Jiangnu stood anxiously at the courtyard wall listening
to the Emperor's soldiers stomping down the road. For months they
had been rounding up workers to build the Great Wall, hundreds of
miles away. *Bang! Bang!* The soldiers' spears pounded on every door.

Meng shuddered, thinking of the men who would soon be taken from their families to toil endlessly. At least her husband would be spared. Wan was a scholar. Scholars were not expected to work with their hands.

Bang! Bang! The hammering was here. A soldier thrust himself into the courtyard and grabbed the servant boy. "You are ordered to work at the Great Wall. Bring me your master."

"I am here." Wan walked slowly across the courtyard.

"You must come too," said the soldier. Meng wept silently as they took her husband away.

All through the autumn Meng waited for news of Wan, but heard nothing. Winter came. Then spring, when the peach trees were dressed with pink blossoms and the swallows flew together to build their nests. And finally summer. Meng's sorrow deepened and her hatred for the cruel Emperor grew.

The following autumn Meng sewed cotton-padded clothing and shoes for Wan to help him bear the biting winter cold up north, but she could not find anyone willing to undertake the long journey to deliver them.

One night a voice called to Meng in her restless sleep. "Wife," said a vision of Wan, his thin body covered with torn clothing, "I am freezing to death."

Meng sprang up to embrace him, and awoke. "I must go to Wan,"
she cried out.

At dawn she slung the bundle of clothing over her back and crossed the courtyard to say good-bye to her husband's parents.

They were stunned. "Good daughter-in-law," said Wan's father, "you have never been away from home one night in your whole life. A woman cannot travel alone. You cannot walk a single mile, much less hundreds of miles," he insisted. "And you travel against fierce autumn winds. Soon snow and ice will cover the mountains."

"Kind father-in-law, I am aware of these perils and thank you for your deep concern, but I must go."

Tears dropped down her mother-in-law's face. "Brave child, we shall await your return."

Meng bowed and left, making her way to the edge of the village.
Far and wide as she could see, dried grass smothered the landscape.
The morning shadows seemed to stretch forever.

Meng took a deep breath and began walking. Soon her feet ached and her hands burned with the weight of the bundle. But she did not stop.

As the days passed, she walked through forests, crossed barren plains, darted among brambles, climbed mountains, and leaped across rivers. Her delicate hands, trained only to embroider and sew, plucked snails from high grass and pulled roots from the hard earth for food. Her fingers hollowed out shelters in the ground.

Her ears that had only listened for the sound of her husband's voice, heard dust storms when they were whispers, sensed windstorms before they howled, and felt thunder long before it brought the rain.

Mile after mile, day after day, with every step, her mind and senses sharpened, her muscles hardened, and so did her heart against Emperor Qin Shi Huangdi.

One evening Meng lay down to rest in a valley. When she awakened she was covered with snow. The road was invisible.

A crow swooped down.

Caw! Caw! It flew on a short distance then sat down on the snow in front of Meng, and cawed again. It flapped its wings and flew up into the sky.

Meng stretched her arms and spread out her sleeves. Then like the crow, she leaped into the wind. Up, up, higher and higher she rose.

Meng flew north. Below, the Great Wall stretched across deserts, wound through plains and grasslands, snaked along rivers, and scaled mountains.

When Meng felt solid earth again she stood before a huge wall that stretched like a dragon from the hills down to the sea. Her journey was over.

Meng walked along the Great Wall, asking the workers if they knew where her husband was.

A worker approached her.

"Our brother Wan, so young and slight, did work here with us. But he was unaccustomed to heavy labor and died from toil."

Meng's eyes widened and stared blankly. "Pray tell me where he lies," she whispered.

"We buried him with hundreds of others in a section of the wall near the sea," the man said, pointing.

But where? Meng searched the length of the wall down to the sea. Anger swelled behind her eyes and forced back the tears. And in their place rage erupted and rose like a tornado to the heavens, forcing the lightning to split the sky.

Rain pounded the bricks, and they trembled and shook. For miles, whole lengths of the Great Wall shattered, releasing the bleached remains of the men who had labored to build it. The wind whipped their bones about.

Meng pricked her finger. "Let my blood penetrate the bones of my beloved," she shouted over and over again, stumbling over skulls and pieces of the wall.

Finally she came to a place where her blood soaked into a pile of bones. Carefully she folded the bones into the bundle of Wan's clothes. "Now I will return home and give you a proper burial."

But hardly had Meng tied the bundle when soldiers appeared and dragged her off to the Emperor.

"Who are you and why have you destroyed my wall?" The Emperor's voice shook with rage.

Meng lowered her eyes and told him of her journey to bring warm clothes to her husband. But the Emperor saw nothing but her beauty.

"Because of my great kindness," he said, "I offer you a choice: Either give yourself to me or I will have you beheaded."

Meng thought for a moment.

"Enlightened One," Meng said, bowing deeply, "I will do as you ask if you grant me three wishes. Without them I prefer to die now."

"What are these three things?" barked the Emperor.

"First, bury my husband as if he were a prince, with gold and jade. Second, have the entire kingdom mourn him for forty-nine days. Third, give him a public funeral."

The Emperor was eager to have Meng for his own. He proclaimed the kingdom in mourning. He instructed his cabinetmakers to build a gold coffin lined with jade, and his masons to make an altar forty-nine feet high, near the sea.

On the forty-ninth day of mourning, the Emperor and his court gathered for Wan's funeral service. Meng stood before Wan's altar, bowed to the Emperor, and thanked him and his ministers for honoring Wan. Then she thanked her parents and in-laws for all their kindnesses.

Then she faced the court. "I have pledged myself to the Emperor, but I must renounce my vow. Emperor Qin Shi Huangdi has destroyed millions of families. He has taken our brothers and fathers and husbands and sons from us, and worked them to death.

"Now I will go where this tyrant cannot touch me." And before the Emperor or any member of his court could move, Meng wrapped her skirt of white silk over her face and leaped into the sea.

The Emperor shouted in fury, "Drag her from the sea. Cut her body into pieces and grind her bones to dust."

His soldiers did his bidding. But when they threw the dust into the sea it turned into thousands of little silvery fish. Today, where the Great Wall meets the Eastern Sea, people watch the silvery fish and remember Meng Jiangnu. They remember her courage and take courage themselves.